We need
a growly lion
and a stripy tiger.

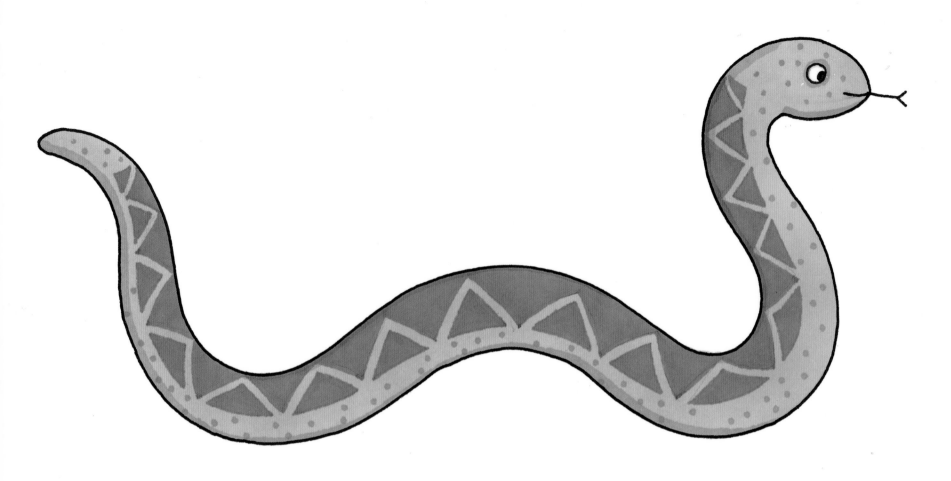

We need
a slithery snake
and an enormous elephant.

We need
a spotty leopard
and a scary gorilla.

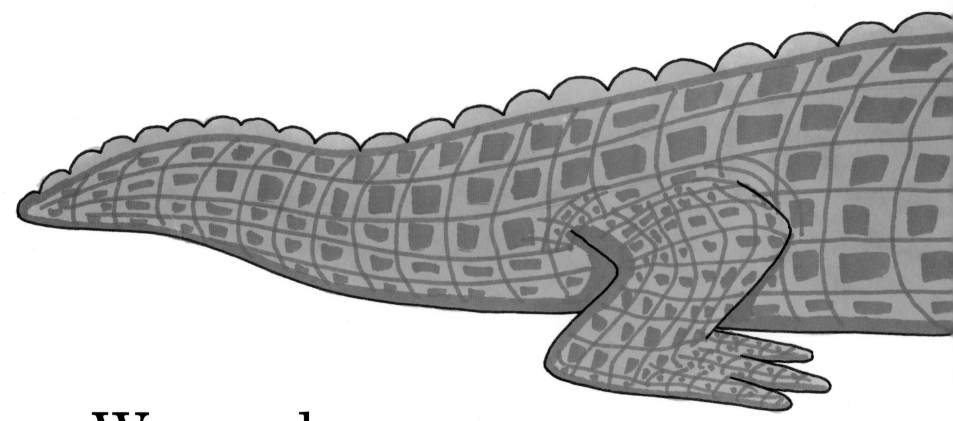

We need
a *very* scary crocodile.

We need
some pretty parrots.

We need
lots and lots
of noisy monkeys.

And we need
jumpy frogs, flappy bats
and all kinds of
creepy crawlies.

Why do we need

some long and tall

a growly  and a stripy

a slithery  and an enormous

a spotty  and a scary

a *very* scary

some pretty  and lots and lots of noisy

jumpy  flappy

and all kinds of creepy crawlies?